Nature's Paintbrush

THE PATTERNS AND COLORS AROUND YOU

WRITTEN AND ILLUSTRATED BY

Susan Stockdale

Simon & Schuster Books for Young Readers

SIMON & SCHUSTER BOOKS FOR YOUNG READERS
An imprint of Simon & Schuster Children's Publishing Division
1230 Avenue of the Americas, New York, New York 10020

Book design by Paul Zakris
The text for this book is set in 16-point Serif Gothic extra bold.
Printed and bound in Hong Kong
First Edition
10 9 8 7 6 5 4 3 2 1

LIBRARY OF CONGRESS CATALOGING-IN-PUBLICATION DATA
Stockdale, Susan.
Nature's Paintbrush: the patterns and colors around you /
written and illustrated by Susan Stockdale.
p. cm.
Summary: Simple text and bright pictures explain the many
uses of colors and patterns in the natural world.
ISBN 0-689-81081-4
1. Color-variation (Biology)—Juvenile literature. 2. Pattern perception—
Juvenile literature. 3. Protective coloration (Biology)—Juvenile literature.
[1. Color. 2. Pattern perception. 3. Camouflage (Biology)] I. Title.
QH401.S67 1999 578.4—dc21 97-46736 CIP AC

NOTES FROM THE AUTHOR/ILLUSTRATOR

ACKNOWLEDGMENTS:
I thank Karen Kearns of Zoo Atlanta, Dr. William R. Stott Jr. of Georgetown University, Dr. Lawrence A. Wilson of Fernbank Science Center, and Ann Edmonds and Jean Norton of The Galloway School for their kind assistance.

ABOUT THE ARTWORK:
First I create a detailed pencil drawing for each image. Then I trace each drawing onto 2-ply Bristol paper, and execute it in acrylic paint. The flat, almost "silkscreenlike" appearance of my illustrations is a result of multiple applications of each color of paint, and the fine detail is the result of using very small brushes and a steady hand.

For Todd, my best friend and
husband extraordinaire

Have you ever noticed the patterns and colors on plants and animals? Patterns may be bold like the stripes on a tiger or beautiful like the feathers of a peacock's tail. Colors may be subtle like the winter white of an arctic fox or radiant like the ruby red of a rain forest frog. But no matter what they look like, patterns and colors are always useful. They help living things survive.

Have you ever touched a starfish? A pattern of hard, round bumps makes its back so rough that few creatures will try to eat it.

Have you ever been pricked by a cactus? Cacti are covered with rows of sharp spines that shield them from hungry desert animals, like the collared peccary.

Have you ever seen a poison dart frog? Their bright colors warn tarantulas and other rain forest creatures that they're deadly to eat.

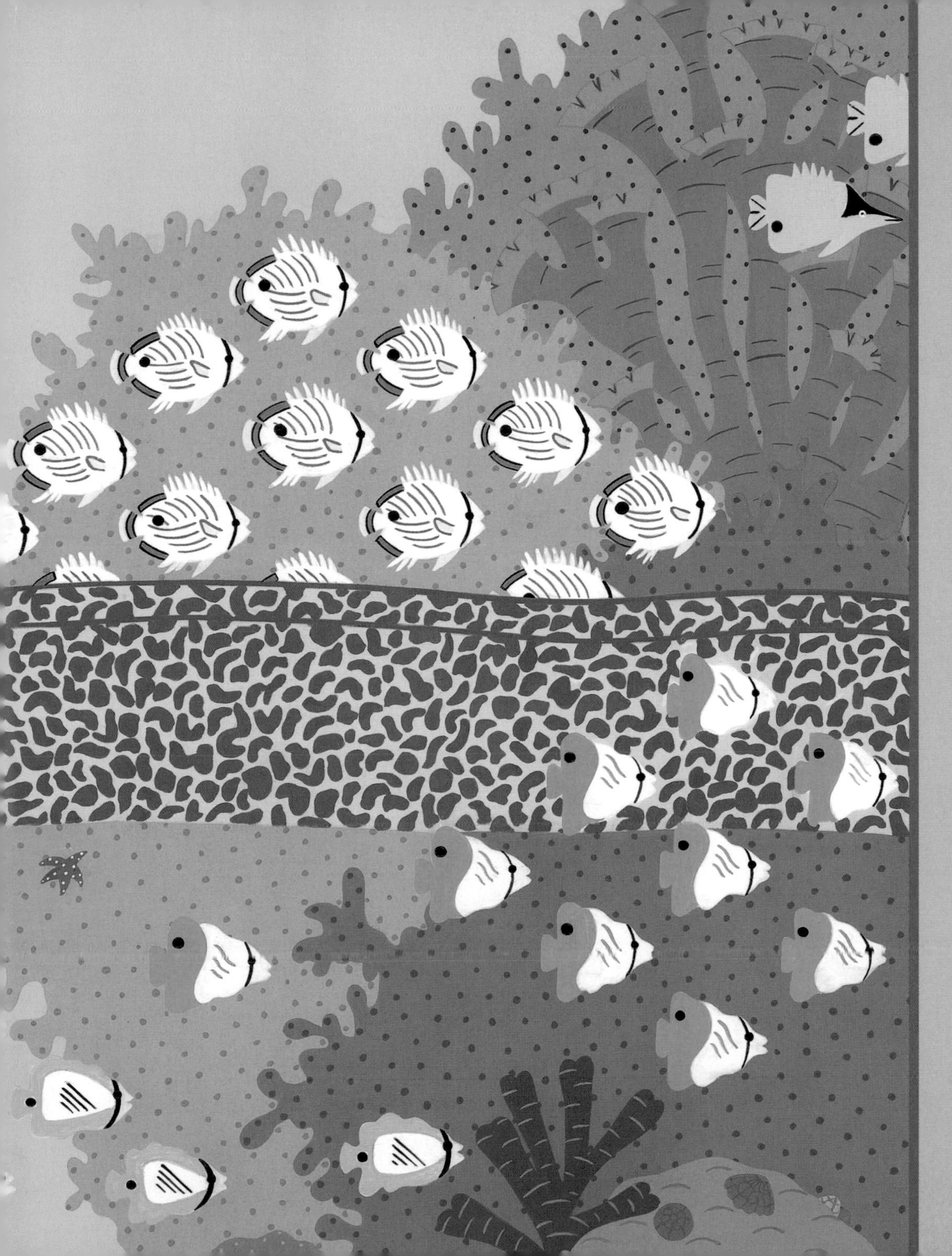

Have you ever noticed the "eyespot" near the tail of a butterfly fish? This false eye confuses the fish's enemies, so they can't tell its head from its tail. If an eel attacks the tail, the fish has an extra moment to escape.

Have you ever found a katydid, almost invisible on a green leaf? Their shape and color match the leaves beneath them, helping these insects hide from birds that like to eat them.

Have you ever watched a tiger weave through tall, waving grasses? Because its stripes are curvy, it blends with its surroundings. On soft, padded paws it creeps up on prey, unseen.

Have you ever seen an arctic fox in winter? Its thick, furry coat is pure white like the arctic snow.

But by summer, its fur is brown, the color of the bare, rocky ground around it. It changes color by shedding its old coat and growing a new one, so in every season it's camouflaged from predators and prey in its northern home.

Have you ever looked at the mottled skin of a rattlesnake?
Curled among the leaves, the snake blends with the forest floor.
If an enemy threatens, the snake's skin pattern also helps it move
since the scales overlap, allowing it to stretch and slide easily.

Have you ever spied a spider spinning its web? It weaves a network of sticky strands to snare insects, then wraps its victim in a silky cocoon to eat later.

Have you ever noticed that flower petals often grow in a circle? This circular pattern directs bees to the flower's center, where they can suck up the sweet nectar they need to make honey, and drop bits of pollen the plant needs to make seeds.

Have you ever spotted a toucan waving its brilliant bill? The male and female birds use their rainbow-colored beaks like flags to attract each other during courtship.

Have you ever seen a peacock show off his dazzling feathers? He spreads them into a fabulous fan to charm a peahen. If she likes his display, they'll become mates.

Everywhere we look, we see nature's wonders. From the shore to the desert to your own backyard, a wide variety of patterns and colors await your discovery. Look closely and see for yourself just how they may be useful to animals, to plants, and even to you.